# Sci-Fi
## stories

Mary Chapman
Alan Durant
David Orme
Gillian Philip

Evans

Published by Evans Brothers Limited
2A Portman Mansions
Chiltern St
London W1U 6NR

*Shades Shorts: Sci-Fi Stories* © Evans Brothers Limited
2009
*The Changeling* copyright © Gillian Philip 2009
*Space Junk* copyright © David Orme 2009
*Strangers* copyright © Mary Chapman 2009
*The Neronian Box* copyright © Alan Durant 2009

First published in 2009

British Library Cataloguing in Publication Data
 Sci-fi stories. - (Shades shorts)
   1. Science fiction, English 2. Young adult fiction,
English
   823'.08762080914[J]

  ISBN-13: 9780237536190

Editor: Julia Moffatt
Designer: Rob Walster

# Contents

# The
# Changeling

# The Changeling

by Gillian Philip

'It's a very primitive life form.' Dr Balthazar tugged his glasses down his nose and eyed it. 'Barely evolved.'

'Look who's talking,' muttered Kit out of the side of his mouth.

I nudged Kit to shut him up.

The thing in the tank. How would I describe it? If you can imagine a lump of animated lard, you'd be nearly there. Or an

# Sci-Fi
## stories

opaque white jellyfish, but with no personality at all. Not even jellyfish personality.

The tanks were set into the wall so that only one side of them was exposed. The glass was the very expensive non-reflective kind, so you could see the exhibits clearly, but it was a bit unnerving. Some of the exhibits had big DANGER DO NOT TOUCH stickers, but you wouldn't think the glass was there till you tapped it.

Which Kit did.

The thing inside didn't seem to react. Maybe the lardy blob pulsed a bit faster, like its heartbeat had speeded up, but as it didn't have a heart that didn't seem likely. Gently Kit rapped the glass again.

'MISTER Castleman!'

Kit yelped and snatched at his finger, but that was only a reflex. It wasn't like he could get the clamp off. I glanced nervously at my own left forefinger, and the little metal clamp fused onto it and screwed into the bone.

Yikes, poor Kit. Despite all his curiosity, he never learned. Balthazar did not like indiscipline, and he was a lot faster to use his own Corporal Correction system than the other teachers. They used it when they absolutely had to, and they didn't like it. Balthazar loved it. He got a kick out of it. You could tell.

Kit whimpered through his teeth, and I squeezed his arm sympathetically.

'I won't have inattention,' said Balthazar coldly. 'See me after class.'

Kit shivered. 'See me after class' meant ten more shocks with the Corporal Corrector. I knew that because I'd got it myself once, for arguing with Balthazar about string theory. *For the last time, boy, I don't want debate. I want PERCENTAGES.*

Which he got, of course. Balthazar's results were always top of the league. Parents clamoured to send their brightest children to him. If only they knew.

Actually, maybe they did. The school system was *very* competitive.

'DiMarco, pay attention!'

I stiffened with terror. Balthazar's pale eyes were fixed on me, and my forefinger itched with fearful anticipation, but no shock came. Kit always got the worst of it. He was too inquisitive and too argumentative.

'It's what, DiMarco?' Balthazar rapped his stick on the tank glass.

'I don't know, sir.'

'Idiot boy. A *chimaera*, DiMarco, or in the common parlance a *changeling*. And never let me hear you use the common parlance.'

11

His eyes glittered. 'What is it, DiMarco?'

'A chimaera, sir – *ow!*'

'Don't try to be clever, DiMarco. What is a chimaera? What does it *do?*'

I couldn't answer. Still trying to get my breath back. The pain in my hand had subsided but it still throbbed. It was just a small charge. A warning.

'The chimaera.' Balthazar drew out his little probe. 'Highly dangerous. Yet it has no intelligence. No memory. A very basic nervous system. Step back, please.'

Hastily we shuffled back. I'd swear the blob flinched away, wobbling into the far corner of the tank.

Balthazar pressed his face to the glass, banged it with the palm of his hand.

'No response, you see? But it does have sensory awareness of a primitive kind.' He slid his probe into the little hole at the top left of the tank and touched it to the blob.

It didn't make a sound, but it shrivelled. Beside me Kit stiffened. The probe worked along the same lines as the Corporal Correctors, we knew that. Kit's fists clenched, but Balthazar pressed the probe harder. The Chimaera trembled and jolted and writhed. I thought if it could squeal, it would really be squealing now.

Balthazar's chilly-scientist look had been replaced by a big grin. He was enjoying himself. And from the way the chimaera had reacted, I realised he'd done this before. A few times, probably. He twisted the probe.

'Sir, stop it!' Kit couldn't contain himself any more.

Balthazar stood up slowly, withdrawing the probe.

'Castleman, your impudence has just

doubled your penalty.' He smirked. 'Tonight you are all to research the chimaera. I want a thousand words by nine o'clock: its native planet, the name of the explorer who discovered it, its properties.'

We scribbled furiously, and headed silently for the library. All but Kit, who slouched after Balthazar. He looked scared, and so he should. But there was something else in the stare he was aiming at the headmaster's shoulder blades.

Looked to me like naked hate.

I knew Kit wasn't asleep. I'd heard him snuffling and gulping when he thought everyone else in the dorm was asleep, but although he was silent now, he hadn't cried himself to sleep. I could make out his shape in the next bunk and he was rigid with tension and fury.

'Kit,' I whispered. 'Did you get to the library? You need the essay in by—'

'Yeah,' came his muffled reply. After a moment he threw off the covers, sat up and glared at me. 'Didn't know you were awake.'

'Just woke up,' I lied. 'What're you doing?'

He was fumbling under his mattress. 'Need to put something back,' he whispered. 'Shut up. Don't let on.' He stood up. He held something in his hand. A scalpel, or a knife.

I rose too.

'Kit, what are you doing?'

'Told you.'

I was scared for him, really scared.

'I'm coming too.'

He stared at me for long moments. 'Okay.'

It wasn't as dangerous as you might think, skulking the school corridors at night. Balthazar thought there'd be no mischief, ever, because we were all so terrified. As a rule he was right.

I frowned as Kit eased open the art room door and tiptoed to the cupboard. Now I knew what he was replacing. It wasn't a knife, it was a glass cutter.

'Kit,' I hissed. 'What's this about?'

He raised a finger to his lips, then beckoned me on. The corridor was in pitch darkness but for tiny lights at floor level. At the swing doors marked *Biology Laboratory – Authorised Persons Only* I stopped.

'Kit,' I hissed. 'We can't go in here.'

'Come on. I've been already. There's no one around.'

He was wrong.

I nearly jumped out of my skin when I saw Dr Balthazar, but I managed to swallow my yelp of terror. His back was turned, and he was leaning against the wall

of tanks, so he hadn't seen us yet. I started
to back away, but Kit seized my arm.

'Wait.'

He crept forward, but Balthazar
didn't move.

Tensing, ready to break into a run
(whatever good that would do me), I
followed. Now I could see Balthazar
properly. His probe was in his right hand,
and his hand was inside the tank. He must
have reached out to tease the Chimaera.

That non-reflective glass. It was so
deceptive and creepy. The tank didn't look
any different now that there was no glass
on the front of it at all. Remembering how
carefully and lovingly Kit had laid the glass
cutter in its drawer, a shiver went down
my spine.

Kit blew out a sigh.

'What a jerk,' he said aloud. 'That's a

17

disappointment. I thought it would happen in class, but the old brute must have come down every night to torment it. Poor little thing. Did you see how scared it was?'

I was trembling, could hardly get the words out.

'Is he... dead?'

'Course he isn't dead,' said Kit scornfully. 'He's in there. Didn't you do your homework?'

He pointed at the tank.

I crept forward as Kit gently manoeuvred the senseless Balthazar out of the way. In the tank, the white lump thrashed and throbbed. It looked furious. It looked as if it was trying to say something.

'Don't touch it!' snapped Kit. 'You want to swap places with the old brute?'

He brought the neatly cut pane of glass from behind a cabinet, eased it back into place, then squeezed a thin line of glass glue round the cut. Pretty amazing work. You wouldn't know it had ever been removed.

Balthazar was blinking and wobbling, coming back to himself. My breath caught in my throat, but he smiled at me and Kit.

'Hank oo,' he said. His lips were a bit floppy and he couldn't speak too clearly.

'You're welcome,' said Kit. 'Poor you. No intelligence indeed. Huh.'

Between us we supported the changeling as it stumbled woozily back to Balthazar's study. Its legs were still very wobbly.

'You'll soon get the hang of it,' said Kit.

'Es,' nodded the changeling. 'Wha 'm I?'

'You're a super headteacher,' said Kit, patting its wobbling back, 'and you've decided to make some serious changes to your school...'

# Space Junk

# Space Junk

by David Orme

'I've got it, Jake. Locking on.'

Slowly, the battered spaceship *Rock On* changed course and moved towards the object floating in space. It would be impossible to see against the huge blue-white-green ball of the Earth below them. But the *Rock On*'s scanners could pick up any object, even if it were just a few millimetres across.

'I think we're close enough,' Jake said. 'Moving the arm out now.'

An arm of steel started to stretch out from the spaceship, guided by Jake on board the *Rock On*. This job needed real concentration.

'Got it. Bringing it in now.'

Jake and Ross were busy guys. They were space garbage men, clearing up the space junk that orbited the Earth. Some of it had been there since space flight started over a hundred and fifty years ago. Some of it fell to Earth and burned up in the atmosphere. Some of it didn't. This was the stuff that was a menace to spaceships.

There had been accidents, bad ones. Spaceships went fast, and hitting even a tiny object was serious. That was why Earth needed space garbage men like Jake and

Ross.

Jake headed down to the garbage hold to see what the arm had brought in. Sometimes it was valuable stuff, lost from a satellite or space station. Most of the time it was just junk.

'It's a spanner, Ross. Some spaceman must have dropped it working outside a space station.'

Ross grunted. Not much money to be made out of a spanner. He switched on the scanner again, sat back, and turned up the music.

Two hours later the scanner pinged again. Ross waited while the computer checked the position of the object. The computer kept a record of everything that was meant to be in earth orbit, from the biggest space station down to the smallest satellite. There was no match. It had to be space junk.

Half an hour later and they were up close. Ross checked the readings again.

'Quite a biggy, this one, Jake.'

'Probably a broken-off solar panel.'

Once more the *Rock On*'s arm reached out to grab. It was a brilliant piece of kit – the end was fitted with strong magnets, and tiny 'fingers' that could hold on to anything.

'Bringing it in.'

The big hatch in the side of the ship opened, and the arm slid neatly inside. The crew heard a thud as the object – whatever it was – was dumped inside. Then the hatch closed. Sensors checked the object for anything dangerous. A light clicked on. Green. All clear. Air was pumped into the hold, and Jake went to see what they had found this time.

'Ross, come and look at this! It's not a

solar panel, that's for sure!'

They could work out what it was, no problem. Airlock door, small windows with light shining out of them, solar panels on the outside. It was a spaceship. Not the same design as they were used to, but a spaceship none the less.

But they had never seen a spaceship that was only a metre long before.

Ross got down on his knees and peered in through the window.

A tiny face peered back at him.

Ross jumped up so fast he banged his head on the roof of the garbage hold, and for a moment he could see stars inside as well as outside the ship.

'There's something in there! Alive!'

Jake didn't believe him, so he had a look. He didn't believe what he saw, so he looked again. This time he saw two faces.

Then a voice, small and squeaky but speaking English, spoke over the ship's radio.

'When you two idiots have quite finished gawking, how about putting us back where you got us?'

Of course, there were always space legends about aliens, and many crazy spaceman had claimed to have seen them. Now Jake and Ross had found some real ones.

'I always thought aliens would be – well, bigger,' said Jake.

'No point in having great lumbering bodies like you lot on Earth. Uses up too much energy, especially if you're going faster than light,' the squeaky voice said.

'You can go faster than light? Wow! Knowing how to do that really would be worth money!' Ross said. 'Can you give us a few clues how you do it?'

'No.'

'Why not?'

'We don't want you lot rushing around the galaxy! You're much too dangerous!'

Jake suddenly thought of something.

'If you are aliens, how come you speak English so well?'

'We've been surveying your planet. We picked it up from your radio and TV. Great TV programmes, by the way.'

Ross was astonished.

'You came all the way across the galaxy just to watch TV?'

'Not just to watch TV. We are looking for knowledge. Fantastic science discoveries, amazing inventions, that sort of thing.'

'Have you found any on Earth?'

'No. But we just love your pop music. Are you into the Martian Maniacs? Great group! Now, will you let us go, please?'

Jake thought about it.

'Say we don't let you go?' he said craftily. 'Say we take you down to Earth? People would pay big money to see you two!'

A small hatch opened in the back of the alien space ship and a metal tube poked out.

'Say we burn a great big hole in your spaceship with our laser cannon?'

'OK, OK, I was just kidding! Let us get back to the bridge and I'll open the hatch.'

'On the other hand, it might just be quicker to burn a hole in your spaceship,' the alien voice said. 'I'm afraid you would get sucked out into space and your bodies would swell up and explode in the vacuum, but I'm sure another garbage ship would come along and clean up.'

The little metal tube started to move up and down, and a humming noise came from inside the spaceship. Ross and Jake went pale.

'Hold on! We'll let you go as soon as we can get out of the garbage hold!'

But the humming noise got louder.

'I like the Martian Maniacs too!' Ross said desperately. 'I've got all their tracks. I'll let you have them if you like!'

The humming stopped. The metal tube disappeared inside the space ship and the hatch clicked shut.

'Have you got *I'm in love with the slimy gal from Pluto*? We're missing that one.'

'Yes! I've got it! As soon as I'm back on the bridge I'll let you download it!'

Ross and Jake rushed out of the garbage hold and sealed the door.

'Quick, find that track before they change their minds!'

'Got it. Are you guys ready?'

'Downloading now,' said the squeaky voice.

Jake opened the garbage hold hatch.

They watched as the tiny spaceship gently nosed its way out and disappeared towards the sun.

'No one will ever believe us,' Jake said gloomily.

'I'm not so sure. They've left us something. While they were downloading that Martian Maniac track, they uploaded a whole lot of stuff. Look! It says here that it's all the best pop music from their own culture.'

'Brilliant! That's bound to be worth money! Play it!'

Ross played the first track.

The two space garbage men looked at each other.

'We've spent the whole of our life looking for garbage...' Ross said

'Yep. And now we've found it,' said Jake. 'Well, what do you expect from Martian Maniacs fans?'

# Strangers

# Strangers

by Mary Chapman

Summer holidays. Boring; all my friends away, not even my brother Ed for company. He'd gone camping with his mates. Mum was at work, as usual.

It was really hot. I was on my way home from the shop, carrying two bags, full of tins of cat food. I trudged along, looking down at the dusty pavement, avoiding the cracks – just in case. Life was dreary enough without inviting bad luck.

'Hi!'

The voice came from the house I was just passing. A girl came down the path. She grinned at me.

'You look fed up.'

I put down my bags.

'Yeah. It's so hot.'

'Would you like a cold drink?'

I hesitated.

'Come on,' she said.

It was almost an order, so I followed her.

'Come into the kitchen,' she said. 'I'll mix us a drink.'

The kitchen was nothing like ours; old-fashioned, no proper units, just shabby cupboards and a bare table in the middle. There was an old camping-stove, a cylinder thing beside it; no microwave or fridge.

The girl took several bottles from a

cupboard, poured stuff from each of them
into two tin mugs, and handed me one.

I took a little sip. It was lukewarm, tasted
sort of herby, but actually quite refreshing.

'I'm Truth,' she said. 'What's your name?'

'Alice... I'm sorry, did you say Ruth?'

'No, Truth.'

'That's a bit – unusual,' I said. It really
was the weirdest name I'd ever heard.

'Beauty is Truth, Truth Beauty,' said
a voice.

A woman stood in the doorway. She
looked exactly like Truth, just slightly older.
Sister?

They both had amazing red hair – long,
curly, masses of it. And they wore similar
clothes; hard to describe. You wouldn't see
them in Topshop, or New Look.

Although it was August they both wore
several layers of tops and long skirts, in

36

muddy swirly colours, as though they'd flung them into the washing-machine with a lot of different coloured dyes. They wore boots as well, and thick coloured tights. Truth's were purple and the woman's were a beautiful soft green.

I realised where I'd seen people before who looked like this – Gran's photos of when she was a hippie. But that was in the sixties, over forty years ago.

The woman came over to me, holding out her arms. I stood up and she hugged me.

'I'm Beauty,' she said.

We don't do hugs in our family, and certainly not with strangers. I wriggled away as soon as I could.

When I looked from one to the other I thought they must be identical twins. But Beauty was definitely older. There were laughter lines at the corners of her eyes, and her hair was grey at the roots.

'Are you Truth's mum?' I asked.

They smiled at each other.

'Yes, and no,' said Beauty.

I felt embarrassed. I shouldn't have asked.

'You look so much like her,' I said.

'Well, I would, wouldn't I?' Beauty said, and they both laughed.

I laughed too, though I didn't see the joke.

'You'll stay for lunch,' said Truth.

'Yes, do,' said Beauty.

'Thank you,' I said. I wasn't sure I wanted to but somehow felt I had no choice. 'That would be nice. There's nobody at home. Mum's at work until six.'

'Good,' said Beauty. 'Now, you girls take your drinks into the garden, while I prepare lunch. It's shady under the trees.'

We sat in the shade though I'd rather have sat in the sun.

'Aren't you a bit hot,' I asked, 'with all those layers?'

Truth looked puzzled.

'No. I need the protection. Why are you wearing so little? You really ought to cover up.'

'It's summer,' I said.

'Exactly,' said Truth.

I didn't know what she meant so I changed the subject.

'Did you move in recently?' I asked.

'Fairly,' she said.

'Where did you live before?'

'Oh, here and there,' she said.

'Which school are you going to in September?' I asked.

She looked puzzled again.

'Which what?' she asked.

'Which school?' It seemed a simple enough question.

'Ah – school,' she repeated. She said it as if it was a foreign language. 'I don't think so.'

That's when I decided they were definitely old-style hippies, maybe squatting, moving around a lot, so Truth didn't go to school. I knew some people didn't send their kids to school but taught them at home. It all added up, even that strange herbal stuff she gave me to drink. They probably hadn't even got a TV or computer.

We had lunch in the kitchen. It would have been nicer in the garden, but neither of them suggested that. They seemed obsessed about keeping out of the sun. It made me hot just looking at them in all those layers of clothes.

I'd prepared myself for peculiar food but it was even worse than I'd imagined. For a start it wasn't very fresh. I'm sure there was mould on my bread, which was horrid and gritty; home-made I suppose. There was soup, mostly potatoes I think. Then a slice of hard greasy cheese (hadn't seen the inside of a fridge) and more bread.

'Thank you,' I said when we'd all finished. 'That was very nice, but I'd better be getting back now.'

'Don't go yet,' said Truth.

'No, stay a bit longer,' said Beauty. 'It's nice for Truth to have company of her own age.'

And they both smiled their identical smiles.

'Come up and see my room,' said Truth.

The room was bare; no bottles, jars, or tubes of make-up, no jewellery or stuff; no TV,

41

computer, CDs or DVDs. A couple of long skirts drooped from wire coat-hangers on the back of the door. There wasn't even a bed, just a sleeping-bag on the floor; beside it a pile of books. I picked up the top one: *Albus Potter and the Fatal Prophecies* – *Albus* Potter?

'It's wonderful, isn't it?' said Truth. 'I've read it six times already. I couldn't wait for it to come out. I can't believe that's the end of the series.'

I flicked it open.

'Haven't you read it?' she asked.

'Not yet.'

I turned over the title page: *First published in Angleland in 2038–*

I dropped the book.

I had to get out of this house.

'Must go,' I said, 'Mum'll wonder where I am.'

'But you said she wouldn't be home until six,' said Truth.

'Could we go out in the garden then?' I asked. 'I need some air.'

Beauty was in the kitchen, making bread, sleeves rolled up, pummelling the dough. From a distance I couldn't see the laughter lines or the grey hair. She looked exactly like Truth. People say I take after Mum but not to that extent. They were identical.

'Just going outside,' said Truth.

I followed her down the path to a bench under an apple tree.

'I hope you don't mind me asking,' I said, 'but is Beauty your mum?'

Truth smiled.

'I've been wondering about you,' she said, 'ever since you asked Beauty that. I guess you are one of the very few remaining

Non-Clones. There aren't many of you left.'

'What are you talking about – Non-Clones?'

I'd vaguely heard of cloning, Dolly the sheep and all that stuff. Science fiction *really*.

'Ninety-five per cent of the population's cloned now,' said Truth, 'since the Twenty-Twenty Act.'

'Twenty-Twenty... what?'

'The Act of 2020 making human cloning compulsory.'

'Compulsory! It's not even legal!'

'You're behind the times, Alice,' Truth said. 'Where've you been?'

'Living my life here and now,' I said, 'not in the year 2020.'

'No, nor me,' said Truth. She laughed. 'I wasn't cloned until 2023!'

'How old are you?' I gasped.

'Fifteen.'

'You're saying this is 2038?' I said. 'It can't be. I'd be forty-four.'

'The same age as Beauty, old enough to be my mother!' said Truth, laughing even more.

'I've got to go,' I said.

I ran back into the house, and through the kitchen. Beauty wasn't there, thank goodness. The front door was closed. I pulled at the handle. It wouldn't move. I shook it. I'd got to get out. I didn't want to be stuck in 2038. I turned to go back to the garden. Maybe I could climb a wall or something. As long as Truth didn't try to stop me.

Beauty came down the stairs.

'Are you going?' she asked.

'Got to feed the cat,' I gasped.

'That's a shame.'

Would she open the door, or not? She

45

leant across me. I thought she was going to grab me, but she only reached across to release the catch on the lock.

'See you later then,' she said, smiling.

I nodded but I was concentrating on getting out of the door, down the path and out into the street. I glanced behind me. She stood in the doorway. I could see the brass number: thirteen, glinting in the sun, just behind her mass of red hair.

I started to run. I think she called out to me, but I just kept going.


When Mum asked about the cat food I realised I'd left it at number thirteeen. She insisted I went back to get it.

No way was I going anywhere near that house again. I nipped upstairs to get my purse. I'd just have to buy some more out of my own money.

I walked on the other side of the road on my way to the shop. I didn't even glance at the house. But coming back, still on the opposite pavement, I had a quick peep.

Nineteen, seventeen, fifteen, eleven – that couldn't be right. I double-checked. There definitely wasn't a number thirteen.

Something was wedged against the wall, halfway between numbers fifteen and eleven. I crossed the road. There were two plastic bags, just like the ones I was carrying, full of tins of cat food.

Mum was pleased, though puzzled, when I arrived home with four bags.

Later that evening I asked, as casually as I could, 'Mum, who lives at number thirteen?'

'There isn't a number thirteen,' she said. 'Never has been.'

# The
# Neronian
# Box

# The Neronian Box

by Alan Durant

There had been war on Mundus for ever.
Well, it had been there long before Agon's
birth fifteen years ago, and before his
father's birth too. It had claimed the lives
of both of Agon's parents when he was
barely two years old. He had been brought
up by his grandfather, who spoke sometimes
of a time long past when their world had
lived in peace and the Neronians had been

distant, indifferent neighbours, not the all too present foes they had since become.

Agon had often asked Grandfather Eng about those old times. The world he described was so different from the one that Agon knew. He spoke of trees, bushes, flowers, grass, of walking through fields, on hills or over sandy shores – of fresh air. Agon found these things difficult to imagine despite his grandfather's loving and detailed descriptions. They were sights he had never seen and never would. The Archive Heritage Bank, where images and living sensory data of the past was stored had been destroyed before Agon's birth in one of the most devastating Neronian strikes on Mundus. Now the people of Mundus had to rely on the memories of the Elders for knowledge about the past.

Fresh air was something that Grandfather

Eng recalled with particular fondness.

'You mean you just breathed it in?' Agon once asked, amazed.

'Indeed we did,' his grandfather nodded. 'We walked in it. It was all around us. When the wind blew, we felt it rush through our lungs.'

'But surely it made you ill?' Agon wondered.

'It wasn't poisoned then,' said his grandfather sadly. 'In those days we could walk in the open air, enjoy the great outdoors. We lived above ground then, not in this warren.'

'But we have air,' Agon protested.

'Filtered air,' Grandfather Eng snorted. 'Not the same thing at all.'

The Mundians had had to build a new world underground when the radiation from the frequent Neronian nuclear attacks had made the planet's atmosphere deadly to all living things. It had destroyed the vegetation and all creatures apart from the Mundians themselves – though a good many of them too had perished. But they had continued to defend themselves in spite of their losses and the Neronians had also suffered many casualties.

No one seemed to know just why the war had started. This was something about which Agon had often quizzed his grandfather. He said he believed it had something to do with an insulting remark made by one of the Mundian Rulers to a Neronian Ruler at an interplanetary conference – though he was not sure this was so, and he had no idea what that remark might have been.

'It just seemed to flare out of nothing,' he said. 'One day we lived in peace; the next we were at war. And so we have remained all these years.'

'But has no one tried to make peace?' Agon inquired.

'There is too much bitterness on either side,' his grandfather sighed. 'Both have lost so much and neither will yield. In the eyes of our Rulers, to sue for peace would be a sign of defeat.'

There was no reason to suppose that the war between Mundus and Neron would ever cease. Now and then, however, Agon did wonder how it might be – and what it would have been like to live back in the days before the war. On his bedchamber wall was a picture of a tree, as produced by Grandfather Eng's mindscanner. ('Mundus was famous throughout the galaxy and beyond for its beautiful trees,' Grandfather Eng had told Agon.) It was such an odd-looking thing: the brown wooden trunk, the branches and the green leaves above, so unsymmetrical and seemingly random, such a contrast to the order and exactness of the Mundian world of today. Agon liked the tree, though. It made him smile to look at it. Imagine a world full of extraordinary things like that – things that weren't made but grew as people did.

One morning – and it was a morning that no one on Mundus would ever forget – Grandfather Eng woke him with momentous news.

'The Neronian warships have gone!' he cried excitedly. 'They beamed a message through this morning to say they no longer wished to fight us. The skies above our world are clear. They've gone, Agon, they've gone!' His eyes were teary with joy as he embraced his grandson.

Agon did not know what to think. For a moment, he wondered if he were dreaming, and even when he knew he wasn't, he felt bewildered.

'Why?' was all he could say, as he sat up in his bedpod.

'I don't know,' said his grandfather. 'I've been summoned with the other Elders to a council meeting in the citadel.'

'Take me with you,' Agon begged. 'Please, Grandfather.'

Within an hour they were in the executive transporter depot. Moments later, they had arrived at the citadel itself. Everywhere there was noise and excitement. People shook hands and embraced one another. Everyone was smiling – even the Elders, who were usually so grave, as if weighed down by the knowledge that they were the generation that had caused the war. Now, at last, that burden was lifted. Peace had returned.

While Grandfather Eng joined the rest of the ruling council in the chamber of decisions, Agon sat in one of the data docks, watching newscasts from around the planet.

'It is time to end the war and make peace, say the Neronians,' announced one cast.

'Let the sins and enmities of the past be in the past,' said another.

'This historic day is the start of a new and beautiful era,' declared a third.

There was talk also of a box that had been left by the Neronians. But no one knew what this box contained or why it had been left. Agon was intrigued.

He asked Grandfather Eng about the box when he came out of his meeting.

'I am going now to look at it,' said Grandfather Eng. 'Come with me if you wish.'

Agon did wish. He walked with his grandfather through the inner corridors, to which only members of the ruling council and their guests had access. They alone, through their DNA patterns, could open the frequent security doors along the way.

The box was on a podium in an isolation shell. They looked at it through the transparent walls of a viewing gallery. It wasn't much to look at, thought Agon. It was plain, black, metallic – old-fashioned too with its lock and key. The key was in the lock, waiting to be turned in order to lift the lid and open the box. This was ancient technology – not really technology at all. Even Grandfather Eng thought it odd.

'The Neronians are the most advanced race in our universe,' he said, 'yet they choose to leave a box such as this.'

'When will they open it?' was what Agon wanted to know.

'That is for the Council to decide,' said Grandfather Eng.

'What is there to decide?' Agon persisted.

'The Neronians have been our sworn enemies for many decades,' said Grandfather Eng. 'There are many among us who do not trust them, or their words of peace, or this gift they have left us.'

Over the following days, the box was scanned and x-rayed to discover what it was made of and what lay inside. But the scans were unsuccessful. As Grandfather Eng told Agon, the box was made of some material unknown on Mundus and no equipment was able to uncover its mysteries.

A great debate took place. The council was split in its opinions. Some thought the box should be destroyed and never opened. Some believed it should be opened as a sign of faith in the Neronians' declaration of peace. Others that it should be kept but not opened. Opinion was split likewise among the ordinary populace of Mundus. In domiciles, work-stations and leisure outlets all over Mundus the box, what might be inside it, and what should be done with it was the topic of everyone's conversation.

Grandfather Eng thought the box too dangerous to be opened. He told Agon an ancient, primitive myth about a box in which had been imprisoned all the evils that could plague the world, such as old age, sickness, madness, spite and rage. This box was never to be unlocked. But a vain and foolish woman named Pandora did open it with catastrophic results.

'To open this box, I fear, may be equally disastrous,' Grandfather Eng concluded.

'But that's just an old myth, Grandfather,' Agon argued. 'The world's moved on.'

He was desperate for the box to be opened. A new age was starting, an age of peace – and this box was its symbol. Opening the box would be like the opening of a brighter, happier future.

Eventually a vote was taken in the council and a decision was reached. By a narrow majority, it was decided that the box should be opened and the moment cast live on screens all over Mundus. As an Elder and representative of the ruling council, Grandfather Eng was one of the official witnesses to the opening – and to his great excitement, Agon too was invited. The Rulers wanted all the generations to be represented, Grandfather Eng explained. And now, the moment had come. Agon looked on, mouth open, pulse racing, as the key was turned in the lock, the lid of the box lifted and at last its secrets were revealed. There was a bewildered outtake of breath among the assembled witnesses. Agon, however, made no sound. He just frowned, uncomprehending. At his side, he heard a quiet, desperate sobbing and turned to see Grandfather Eng with tears flowing down his face.

'It's worse than Pandora's box,' he whimpered. 'What greater evil could there be to face than the pain of seeing what you have lost and can never have again?'

Agon looked once more inside the open box, seeing now what his grandfather saw – the loss of a beloved son and daughter-in-law, of so many friends and fellow

Mundians, of a beautiful world of fresh air and natural, growing things all destroyed by war.

In the box the Neronians had left was a single green leaf.